michelle.

GW00857966

SARAH SCRAP
and Her Wonderful Heap!

Wendy Lewis

Cloverleaf
An imprint of Evans Brothers Limited

Published by Evans Brothers Limited
2A Portman Mansions, Chiltern Street
London W1M 1LE

Cover design by Design Revolution, Brighton

© text Evans Brothers Limited
© illustrations Wendy Lewis

Story written by Su Swallow
Illustrations by Wendy Lewis. The idea for this story and the character
of Sarah Scrap was created by Wendy Lewis and is her copyright.

All rights reserved. No part of this publication may be reproduced,
stored in a retrieval system, or transmitted, in any form or by any
means electronic, mechanical, photocopying or otherwise, without
prior permission of Evans Brothers Limited

First published 1990

Typeset by Fleetlines Typesetters Ltd., Southend-on-Sea
Printed in Hong Kong by Wing King Tong Co. Ltd.

Cased edition ISBN 0 237 51152 5
Limp edition ISBN 0 237 51178 9

There was once a grey town full of grey houses, where the sky was often dull and grey. Sometimes even the people that lived there felt dull and grey. They longed for some colour in their lives, but they were too busy to notice when a patch of bright green appeared in the middle of their town.

Life was often dull for the children in this grey town, even in the holidays. They longed for adventure but did not know where to look.

One day Emma spotted a butterfly and decided to follow it. "Come on, you lot," she said. "Let's see where it lands. I'll race you." The butterfly seemed to wait, then it flew off.

The children chased after the butterfly, running and skating as fast as they could. Once or twice the butterfly seemed to wait for them, then it flew off again.

The butterfly led them to a wasteland, where it landed on an old sofa.

"I won!" the children all shouted at once.

They did not notice when a strange little lady appeared beside a patch of bright green grass.

The strange little lady called the children over. "I'm Sarah Scrap," she said. "Glad you got my invitation."

"What invitation?" asked Emma, but Sarah Scrap just flapped her arms and smiled.

"A little butterfly told me you are looking for adventure," said Sarah. "Come back tomorrow and I will show you some treasure."

"Maybe," said the children, who decided Sarah was odd but nice.

Sarah Scrap disappeared into the little hill where she lived. Inside, there was rather a mess. She decided to tidy up, ready for her visitors. So she . . .

. . . sorted out the newspapers . . .

. . . put all the empty bottles in neat rows. . .

. . . stacked up the tin cans.

When it was all tidy she made some rose-hip tea and . . .

. . . fell into bed.

"What a wonderful heap this is!" she said.

"I knew you'd come," said Sarah Scrap when the children arrived the next day. "Welcome to my treasure trove."
The children looked round at the piles of newspapers and the rows of bottles.
"Treasure?" said Max. "Looks more like a rubbish museum!"
"Exactly. Precisely. Got it in one," said Sarah Scrap. "Other people's rubbish is Sarah Scrap's treasure!"

"I knew it!" muttered Max. "No treasure, no adventure. Silly old Sarah." Sarah shook her plaits, flapped her arms and sat down. "Now listen," she said. "This rubbish is worth saving. It can all be turned into new things — new paper, new glass, new plastic, new metal. It can all be recycled. Wish I could be! Ha! Anyway, come outside and I'll show you some more rubbish that's worth saving. Waste not, want not, what?"

"Not a pretty sight, is it?" said Sarah. "Let's start sorting. Remember: if it's useful, don't Sarah Scrap it, **Sarah SAVE it!**"

So the children sorted and sifted and stacked the rubbish. They found some interesting things, and got rather dirty.

"Come back tomorrow, won't you?" said Sarah. "There's more!"

The children did come back the next day, and the next, and the next.

When all the rubbish was sorted and sifted and stacked it was time to take it away. So the children took . . .

. . . the bottles to the bottle bank . . .

. . . the cans to the can bank and . . .

. . . the newspapers to the paper mill.

A lorry took the skip full of
real rubbish to the tip.

The wasteland was clear at last.
"Bring forks and spades tomorrow," said Sarah.

"Now what?" asked the children the next day.

"Now this," said Sarah, pointing to some plants. "Now we will make a garden where you can play. Let's get digging!"

The children dug — and dug. Small holes for seedlings, bigger ones for trees and a giant hole for a pond.

"Come back tomorrow," said Sarah. "I have a surprise for you."
"We know all about Sarah's surprises," said Max with a smile.

The next day, Sarah's surprise surprised even Max.
''Follow me,'' she said. So the children followed her across the wasteland and over her heap to a patch of bright green.

''This is my wild garden,'' said Sarah. ''Your wasteland will be like this one day. Full of snails and spiders, frogs and fish, birds and butterflies. From wasteland into wonderland. Ha!''

All the children were surprised at how quickly their wasteland changed into a wild garden. The grass grew green, the flowers bloomed and all kinds of animals moved in. And the children had a good place to play in. They got very cross if anyone left any rubbish lying about. "Don't Sarah Scrap it, Sarah SAVE it!" they said. But where was Sarah Scrap?

The children ran over the hill to Sarah Scrap's wonderful heap. "Let's ask her to come on a picnic," said Emma. But they were too late. Sarah Scrap was leaving town. "Time I was off," she said. "Lots to do — more rubbish to rescue, and all that. Be kind to butterflies, won't you? Ta ta!"
And then Sarah disappeared between the grey buildings.

The children decided to take a last look inside Sarah's wonderful heap.
"Pity to waste this," said Emma. "Let's start our own treasure trove."

So the children collected all kinds of interesting things: old bottles, books, bits of cars and lots of other things. "Perhaps we could open a museum of rubbish!" said Max.

Perhaps Sarah is on her way to your town now. Look out for the butterfly . . .